The Suite Life of Zack & Cody

Check It Out

May 2007

Adapted by Beth Beechwood

Based on the television series, "The Suite Life of Zack & Cody", created by Danny Kallis & Jim Geoghan

Based on the episode written by Marc Flanagan

New York

Chapter 1

Life at the Tipton Hotel was almost never dull, but today felt pretty boring to Zack. He had a science project to work on with Cody, but that was pretty much the last thing he wanted to do. As he and Cody waited for the elevator in the lobby, Zack tried not to think about the tedious work that awaited him upstairs. He focused on his yo-yo skills, instead. When the elevator doors opened,

Cody stepped in, but Zack just kept playing with his yo-yo. Cody stared at his brother. "Hey, come on, man," he whined to Zack. "We have to go work on our science project."

"I *am* doing science," Zack explained as he threw the yo-yo out in front of himself for the "around the world" trick. "Look, centrifugal force."

Cody had no choice—he would have to go up and start the project himself. His brother was of no use to him right now, anyway.

Zack continued to play with the yo-yo after the elevator doors closed. He was sure Cody could handle the science project by himself.

Meanwhile, London had entered the hotel in a huff. She and her dog, Ivana, were both wearing party hats. As ridiculous as this might have looked on someone else, London managed to carry it off with some degree of authority. Maybe because she also had on a fur shrug and light green–tinted sunglasses. She was the picture of trendiness. She crossed over to the candy counter where Mr. Moseby was having tea and chatting with Maddie.

"Moseby!" London shouted. She clearly had an agenda and was in no mood for small talk. "Jeny Freiberger just threw the most incredible party for her dog, and Ivana's upset."

"Of course she is." Maddie couldn't resist. It had to be said. "Look at that stupid hat you put on her." London was a good friend, but Maddie enjoyed making fun of her in spite of that fact.

"Cat person," London replied, barely giving Maddie's comment a thought. She was used to Maddie's snide comments about the way she dressed Ivana. She turned her attention back to Mr. Moseby; she knew he would take care of this for her. He had to do what she said: her father was his boss, and Mr. Moseby *lived* to please his boss. "I want a bigger, better party for Ivana, in the grand ballroom. Here's the guest list," she said, handing him a piece of paper.

"I will take care of it personally," Mr. Moseby said. Just as quickly as she had come, London was gone. Mr. Moseby handed the list to Maddie. "Maddie, take care of it personally," he said.

Maddie sighed. She always got these kinds of jobs. "No one else will touch it?"

"Not with a ten-foot pooper-scooper," Mr. Moseby replied.

Just then, Esteban ran up to them, waving a piece of paper. "Mr. Moseby! You received a fax! The Tipton Hotel inspector is on the way for a surprise inspection."

Mr. Moseby wasn't terribly concerned. "How can it be a surprise inspection if they sent a fax?" he asked.

"Because the fax came two weeks ago, and I forgot to give it to you. Surprise!" Esteban said meekly. He was always so eager to please his boss, but this time he had screwed up. He felt terrible. Luckily, Mr. Moseby relieved him of his guilt immediately.

"Fortunately for all of us, my hotel is always in tip-top Tipton shape, and nothing has changed since the last inspection." But not everything was the same as last time. Just as Mr. Moseby finished his sentence, a certain yo-yo came sailing through the air, landing smack in his teacup. With tea splashed across his face, Mr. Moseby glared at Zack and said, "Except for that."

Without realizing it, Zack had reminded Mr. Moseby of exactly what had changed. He made a run for it.

Cody was busy working on his science project at the kitchen table, when Carey entered the room. Muriel, the hotel maid, was cleaning around them.

"Hey, Muriel," Carey asked with some concern. "When you were cleaning in the bedroom, did you see a five-dollar bill?"

"I thought you were throwing that out," Muriel said earnestly.

Carey, knowing who she was dealing with, said, "It was on my dresser." Muriel could be exasperating sometimes.

"My bad," Muriel said matter-of-factly as she handed Carey the bill. Carey eyed the maid, but before she could consider her exchange with Muriel, Zack burst in, huffing and puffing.

"Hide me!" he shouted.

"Whoa, whoa, whoa!" Carey slowed her son down. "What happened?"

"Moseby's after me! Just because I was playing with my yo-yo in the lobby, and it might have landed in his mug."

"And then?" Carey asked.

"I ran after that," Zack admitted. "He scares me."

"Mr. Moseby is just doing his job. He needs to keep this hotel running smoothly, and you tend to be . . ." Carey paused for a moment, trying to think of the right word. "Unsmooth," she finished, smiling.

"Yeah, unsmooth like Mom when she doesn't shave her legs for two weeks," Cody joked.

Carey wasn't amused. Her mouth was agape at her son's comment. "Aren't you two supposed to be working on your science experiment?"

"We've already started. Look!" he said, opening the cabinet. Inside were two cages, each with a rat inside. Carey was so horrified, she jumped up on a chair and started screaming hysterically.

"Aaaaaaaaahhhhhhhhh! No, no, no! What . . . what are you doing with those rats?"

"Science," Zack replied, as if it were *so* obvious.

"We got these from our school," Cody explained further. "This is Bonnie, and that's Clyde. They're our experiment."

"Which is what?" Carey said, still shaky. She stepped off the chair, cautiously. "Giving your mother a heart attack?"

"No, I play rap music for Bonnie and heavy metal for Clyde, and then Cody writes down some scientific stuff."

"You know, behavioral changes . . . like eating habits, mood swings, urination patterns—"

Carey interrupted him. "Ewww! Why does it have to be rats?" She was wiping herself all over, trying to get the grossness of the situation off.

"Too late now," Zack said. "We've bonded." He hugged one of the cages affectionately.

"Swell," said Carey, picking up the cages. "Well, if you don't mind, I'm going to take Bonnie and Clyde away from where we eat." She was carrying the cages with just two fingers, holding them as far away from herself as possible. When she was gone, the doorbell rang.

"I'll get it," Cody said.

"No, wait. What if it's Mr. Moseby? I'm toast."

Cody thought about that for a second. He decided he had no problem with that scenario. "Come in!" Cody shouted happily. Mr. Moseby entered their suite with a big smile on his face. Zack immediately felt the need to explain himself.

"Look, Mr. Moseby, about that yo-yo—"

But for once, Mr. Moseby didn't seem mad . . . at all. "Oh pish-posh," he said with a little too much enthusiasm in his voice. "Boys will be boys. You were just having fun, and that's what boys do, isn't it? They have fun!"

Zack stared at Mr. Moseby. Had he gone crazy? "Did that yo-yo bounce off your head?"

"No. I'm fine. I came up here to offer you scamps tickets to today's Red Sox game. It's a matinee." Mr. Moseby handed the boys the tickets, and they couldn't contain themselves. They actually jumped up and down!

"The Sox game?!" Cody yelled. "All right!"

"Yes, and your seats are just above that little hut wherein the players spit and scratch themselves," Mr. Moseby said. Now Zack was suspicious. This just didn't add up. Only a few minutes ago, he had splashed Mr. Moseby in the face with hot tea. Now, the man was giving them Sox tickets—right above the dugout. Something was up.

"Hold on. There's something wrong here," Zack insisted.

"Why do you question my generosity?" Mr. Moseby asked, clearly trying to cover something up.

"Yeah," Cody said to Zack, waving the tickets in front of his brother's face in hopes that he wouldn't ruin this for them. "Why *do* you question his generosity?" He glared at Zack.

"I'll tell you what," Zack said to Mr. Moseby, with a plan in mind, "you go. I think I'll just stay here and hang out in the ol' lobby. Where's my model rocket?" There was no way Mr. Moseby would let that happen. He had to give it up now.

"No! All right, fine," he conceded. "The hotel inspector will be arriving soon, and it would be marvelous if you weren't around," he admitted.

"I knew it!" Zack exclaimed. He loved it when his instincts didn't let him down. He considered his situation for a moment. He was pretty sure he had some leverage here. "We'll be 'not around' longer if you throw in a little money for dinner," he said. The boys left Mr. Moseby no choice. He knew what he was up against. He reached into his pocket and handed them some cash.

"I like lobster," Cody said.

Mr. Moseby sighed and handed them more cash. The deal was done—his hotel's reputation was safe. He could breathe a big sigh of relief . . . or at least he thought he could.

Chapter 2

Cody and Zack were in their room, excitedly getting ready to go to the big game. As Cody grabbed their mitts, he noticed Zack taking Clyde out of his cage. "What are you doing?" he asked.

"I'm taking Clyde to the game," Zack said to Cody, as if it was perfectly reasonable to bring a rat to a baseball game.

"You can't do that, it'll contaminate the

experiment. Who knows what 'Take Me Out to the Ball Game' will do to his urinary pattern?"

"Fine," Zack said as he put the rat back in his cage. "But this is why they like me more than they like you."

Their mother called to them, "Come on, guys! If we make batting practice, I might meet a player!" Cody hurried out of the room and Zack followed him until he heard a squeaking noise he couldn't resist.

"Okay, I'll take you," he said to Clyde as he pulled the rat out of his cage, "but don't tell Cody." He stuffed Clyde into his coat pocket. Only the squeaking didn't stop. Apparently, Bonnie wasn't too pleased with this arrangement. "Oh, sorry, Bonnie. I didn't know you'd want to go, too," he said, pulling her out. "How sexist of me!" Carey wouldn't have been pleased about excluding

Bonnie, even if she was a rat. He put Bonnie in his other pocket and headed out to the game.

In the lobby, the staff was making sure the hotel was at its best. Mr. Moseby walked up to Esteban, who was gluing a vase to the table in the middle of the lobby. Mr. Moseby was getting more anxious by the minute. It was getting late, and the hotel inspector had not yet arrived. He had gone to all the trouble of getting rid of the twins, and now there was a very real possibility that they would be present for the inspection anyway. The idea of this made Mr. Moseby jittery. "When is the hotel inspector going to be here?" he asked Esteban. "Zack and Cody are going to be back any minute."

"Oh, don't worry, Mr. Moseby. Per your instructions, I am gluing down the vase. Soon, it will be twinproof," Esteban reassured his boss, as if the vase were the only thing in the hotel the twins could possibly destroy.

While Mr. Moseby paced in nervous anticipation of the inspector's arrival, London and Maddie were discussing Ivana's party over at the candy counter. Or rather, London was discussing Ivana's party while Maddie pretended to care.

"I have the most fantastic idea for Ivana's party," London said.

"Canceling it?" Maddie suggested hopefully. She'd have given anything not to have to plan this ridiculous party.

"Don't be silly. I saw this fabulous painting of dogs playing poker." She paused for dramatic effect. "Ivana wants a poker party."

"You do know those dogs weren't really playing poker?" Maddie asked incredulously. It seemed to her that London hadn't quite thought this through.

"If they weren't playing poker, how did that Dalmation win all the money, huh?"

Apparently, she *had* thought it through—she had simply come to the wrong conclusion. Maddie resigned herself to planning the silly doggie poker party. "Poker party it is," she said. Satisfied, London walked away, bumping into Mr. Moseby on her way. Mr. Moseby, who was already feeling shaky, wobbled on his feet. In an effort to steady his boss, Esteban grabbed on to him.

"Thank you, Esteban," Mr. Moseby said. But as he started to walk away, Esteban moved as if glued to him. As a matter of fact, he *was* glued to him! "You can let go now," Mr. Moseby told Esteban.

"I wish I could," Esteban said anxiously. "They don't call it Mega Glue for nothing." And of course, it was at this precise moment that Ilsa Schickelgrubermeiger, the hotel inspector, arrived. A large woman with a large name, she had a large mole on her face to match. She was imposing in her pin-striped suit, her hair in braided buns. In fact, she was more than imposing, she was . . . threatening. She approached Mr. Moseby.

"Mr. Moseby?" she said with a thick accent.

Trying as hard as he could to free himself from Esteban's clutches, Mr. Moseby waved his arms frantically, but to no avail. Esteban went everywhere he went. "That's right," he replied to the woman. "May I help you?"

"I am Ilsa Schickelgrubermeiger, the Tipton Hotel inspector."

"Yes, of course. We were expecting you

hours ago," he said, still trying to get rid of Esteban.

"I got held up at Logan Airport," she said.

"Traffic?" he asked. The traffic from the airport was always brutal.

"No, their whole luggage system stinks. I had to redo it." She was serious.

"Welcome to the Tipton," Mr. Moseby said, extending his arms with Esteban still attached to him.

"Mr. Moseby, do you realize you're wearing a bellhop?" The inspector said this without even the teeniest bit of humor. Mr. Moseby had been too busy staring at the giant, hairy mole on her chin to concentrate on what she was saying. He guessed at an answer.

"It goes with your devastating good looks," he covered.

The hotel inspector was suspicious of Mr.

Moseby's incoherence. "Are you staring at my beauty mark?" she asked.

Mr. Moseby was quick to shout, "No!" But at the exact same time, Esteban shouted, "Yes!" Mr. Moseby was not pleased. He turned to Esteban to reprimand him, "Would you stop that?!"

"Yes, sir!" Esteban said, saluting his boss. Only, his arm was connected to his boss, so the salute didn't show much respect as it hit Mr. Moseby in the face.

"Ow!" Mr. Moseby complained. "Let go!" Esteban knew it was time to sever himself from his boss. He ripped his hands away as hard as he could, and he was free! So was Mr. Moseby—free of his suit sleeves!

Esteban took in his boss's new duds. "Ooh," he said. "I love the vest look on you, sir."

Mr. Moseby stared Esteban down, and Esteban decided it was probably time for him to leave the area, lest there be any more unfortunate incidents. "But like your sleeves, I am off," he said lightly. As he exited, Ilsa the inspector scribbled something in her notebook. Mr. Moseby noticed and was eager to correct her perception of how he ran his hotel.

"If I might explain—" he started to say. But, Mr. Moseby's luck was getting worse by the second now. The twins were back from the Red Sox game. They raced toward Mr. Moseby with giant foam fingers waving, shouting like they were still in the stands at Fenway.

"Hey, Mr. Moseby!" Zack yelled.

"The Sox won ten to nine!" Cody told him.

"And Mom caught a foul ball!" Zack said.

It seemed Carey had caught the foul ball

with her face. She entered the lobby with a big bandage on her forehead. "Yeah," she said. "Apparently 'heads up' means 'heads down,'" she said. Unbeknownst to any of the group, Bonnie and Clyde slipped out of Zack's pockets.

"So, is the evil hotel inspector gone yet?" Zack asked Mr. Moseby.

Ilsa stepped in at this point. "No," she said. "She's right here."

"Whoa!" Zack said, staring at the hard-to-miss protrusion. "What's that on your face?" Tact wasn't exactly Zack's forte. Carey, embarrassed, quickly put her hand over Zack's mouth.

Mr. Moseby's blood pressure was on the rise. Through clenched teeth, he muttered, "It's a beauty mark."

"But it has a hair on it!" Cody remarked, as he studied the inspector's mole.

Carey took this opportunity to put her other hand over Cody's mouth. "It's a good thing I don't have triplets," she joked, "I'm running out of hands. Thanks again for the tickets to the game," she said to Mr. Moseby.

Zack managed to break free of his mother's hand, "Yeah," he said, "I know those tickets are usually for the guests, so we really appreciate it."

At that, the inspector scribbled in her notebook and muttered aloud, "Oh, ignores guests' needs for friends . . ."

Mr. Moseby was quick to correct her, though. "They're not my friends."

This didn't help. She wrote some more. "Oh, ignores guests' needs for strangers. What kind of hotel manager are you?" she asked Mr. Moseby, glaring at him.

Cody had to defend the guy. "He's the

best. He's number one." He and Zack waved their foam fingers in enthusiastic agreement.

"Yeah," Zack said, "last week he let us make s'mores in the kitchen. And then he put the fire out all by himself." He was sure this would prove to the inspector what a great guy Mr. Moseby was, but Carey thought Zack better not say anymore.

"Okay," Carey said, sensing that their presence wasn't helping her boss one bit. She pulled the boys away.

Ilsa Schickelgrubermeiger had a sour look on her face. "Mr. Moseby, I have been here for five minutes and I am not impressed."

"I assure you there won't be any more surprises," Mr. Moseby said with confidence. But he should have known better. Suddenly, a hotel guest screamed and then another followed. And all at once, there was mayhem.

"Eek! A rat!" one guest yelled. "I saw a rat!" Another screamed, "a big rat!"

Mr. Moseby quickly reconsidered his promise to the inspector. "Starting now," he said to her, with a smile. He thought he might as well lighten the mood. Guests were panicking all around them. They were jumping on tables and rushing the exits. Meanwhile, Cody shot Zack a knowing look, while Carey watched the boys suspiciously.

"Mr. Moseby," Ms. Schickelgrubermeiger said with disgust, "in my twenty years as a hotel inspector, I have never been so appalled. Rats in the lobby?"

"But—" Mr. Moseby tried to defend himself once again, but she wouldn't have it.

"Dut-dut-dut!" she scolded, cutting him off. "I am taking over the management of this hotel until a review board arrives to make their final decision." She paused then and held out her hand. "Your Tipton Hotel keys," she demanded. Mr. Moseby had no choice. He reluctantly handed them over.

Zack and Cody looked on, horrified. "Not his keys," Zack moaned.

"Your gold-plated Tipton badge," she said next, and Mr. Moseby handed it over.

"Not the badge," Cody said, cringing.

"Your Tipton tie," she said. Ilsa Schickelgrubermeiger was relentless.

As Mr. Moseby sadly untied his tie and handed it to her, he said, "I feel compelled to disclose that I am wearing custom-made Tipton boxer shorts."

But this woman clearly had no sympathy. "Dry clean them and send them back," she replied sternly. All eyes on Mr. Moseby, he stomped toward the exit in disgust. Mr. Moseby being Mr. Moseby, though, he simply could not walk out without taking in his precious lobby one last time. He stopped at the top of the stairs, took one last dramatic look at the Tipton lobby, and bowed his head sadly. Then, he was gone.

Carey, Zack, and Cody all looked on in disbelief. They couldn't believe Mr. Moseby actually got fired.

"Poor Mr. Moseby," Carey said.

"Yeah, but what are the odds?" Cody replied. "There are two rats downstairs, and we have two rats upstairs."

Carey had a thought she was afraid to share. But she looked at Zack and braced herself. "They are upstairs? Aren't they?" she asked.

Zack had to come clean. "Well . . ." he paused to see his brother and mother glaring at him.

"Oh . . ." Carey said.

Zack told them the truth. "They were in my pockets when we came back from the game. They must have snuck out when we got back to the hotel."

Never mind that Zack had gotten Mr. Moseby in serious trouble, Cody was upset about their school project. "You ruined our science experiment!"

Carey made sure to remind both of them that Zack's antics had other consequences, too. "And more importantly, you may have ruined Mr. Moseby. Zack, you better think about what you just did. You may have cost the man his job."

When it hit Zack what he had done, the guilt set in, too. They all went upstairs and braced themselves for life at the Tipton Hotel . . . without Mr. Moseby.

Chapter 3

A very long week had gone by since the firing of Mr. Moseby, and the staff and guests of the Tipton Hotel were paying a steep price for his departure. Ilsa Schick-elgrubermeiger was making everyone nervous. To make matters worse, Zack and Cody still hadn't located Bonnie and Clyde. This morning, the boys were busy crawling around the couches in the lobby looking for their rats for the zillionth time. They had offerings of gourmet cheese for the furry little rodents, if only they would come back.

"Here, Bonnie. Here, Clyde," Cody coaxed, hoping his science project wasn't as doomed without the rats as the Tipton Hotel was without Mr. Moseby.

"It's been a whole week," Zack moaned. "I don't think this cheese is working."

Ilsa, who was on her usual military-style patrol of the lobby, picked up a piece of Zack and Cody's cheese. "Muriel!" she demanded. It was as if she didn't have a lower voice to use inside. "What is this?"

Muriel popped the cheese in her mouth without a moment's thought. "Mmmm, Gorgonzola. If you want some, there's more under the couch," she said matter-of-factly.

Just then, Ilsa spotted Esteban. "Esteban!" she yelled.

"Yes, sir," he replied. Then, realizing his mistake, he said, "Ma'am."

Ilsa leaned down and peered at the small pin on his vest. "What is that nonregulation pin you're wearing on your Tipton uniform?"

"It belonged to my great-grandfather, who died fighting for my country's independence," Esteban replied with emotion in his voice.

Ilsa tried to be sweet for exactly one second. "How touching," she said. But she was quick not to veer too far from her usual drill sergeant demeanor. "Take it off!" she commanded.

Esteban had no choice but to comply. Ilsa looked at him suspiciously. "I'm watching you," she sneered. Genuinely afraid of his new boss, Esteban whimpered.

Meanwhile, Muriel, Zack, and Cody

had witnessed the whole exchange. "Man," Zack said, "I never thought I'd miss Moseby."

"Yeah, she's a real witch. I'd love to vacuum off that mole," Muriel said with vengeance in her voice.

They all watched as Ilsa approached Maddie at the candy counter. "You there, candy girl," she said.

Maddie, thinking her boss had simply forgotten her name, innocently offered it to her. "My name's Maddie."

As if Ilsa cared. "Yeah, candy girl. I see you punched in at four-o-one. You were supposed to be here at four to work on London's poochie party."

"Sorry," Maddie said. This woman was just nuts.

"Four o'clock means four o'clock. I'm docking you for that minute."

"That's a dime," Maddie observed in disbelief.

"A dime you'll never see!" Ilsa said dramatically, just before she stomped away.

"Man, getting Mr. Moseby suspended is the worst thing we've ever done," Zack said.

"And by *we* you mean *you*?" Cody reminded Zack. There was no way he was going to share the blame for this. He had thought it was crazy to take the rats to the baseball game in the first place.

Zack got serious. "I'm gonna go over there and talk to her. If it doesn't go well, I want you to have my yo-yo." He walked toward Ilsa nervously. "Ms. Schickel . . . geiger . . . counter . . ." He just couldn't get that name right.

"Close enough," she snapped. "What?!" Zack tried to remember what he had wanted to say, but he was fixated on her mole and lost his train of thought. It was so big . . . and so . . . hairy.

"What are you staring at?" Ilsa asked.

Zack snapped out of it. "Nothing," he gulped. "I just wanted to say that the rat thing was not Mr. Moseby's fault."

Again she put on her sweet voice. "Well, that changes things," she said.

Zack was so relieved. "Really?" he asked.

"No!" she shouted. "A manager is responsible for everything that happens in the hotel. The buck stops here! Speaking of which, I want the two of you to stop coming in the front entrance willy-nilly."

Zack couldn't believe this. "But Mr. Moseby always lets us—" he started to protest, but Ilsa was quick to correct him.

"Mr. Moseby doesn't work here anymore," she said.

"But we—" Zack didn't want to give up so easily.

"Dut-dut-dut! End of conversation." Ilsa walked away and that was that. There was just no reasoning with this woman. Zack had to come up with a new plan.

Chapter 4

Later that day, Zack found himself at the door of Mr. Moseby's apartment. Inside, Mr. Moseby was apparently awaiting a pizza delivery because when he heard the doorbell ring, he yelled, "It's been thirty-one minutes! That pizza is free!"

When Mr. Moseby opened the door, he was surprised to find Zack instead of the pizza guy. Meanwhile, Zack was surprised when he saw the inside of Mr. Moseby's apartment. It was decorated exactly like the lobby of the Tipton. Exactly.

"Hello, Mr. Moseby," he said as he looked around.

"Zack," Mr. Moseby said without any feeling whatsoever. He was too busy sucking on a Popsicle to show any emotion.

"Wow! Your apartment looks just like the Tipton lobby," Zack exclaimed.

"It was a two-for-one deal," Mr. Moseby explained self-consciously. "What brings you here?"

"You gotta come back, Mr. Moseby," Zack begged. "Ilsa's a nightmare."

"I'm sorry to hear that, but there is nothing I can do. I have been suspended. Now, I hope you enjoyed your stay at the Moseby apartment," he said as if bidding farewell to a Tipton guest. He tried to shoo Zack out.

"You can't give up. The Tipton is your whole life," Zack pleaded.

"Not necessarily," Mr. Moseby said, clearly trying to convince himself of this. "I have other interests. I've always wanted to learn to drive the big rigs. Breaker-breaker," he said, pretending to man a CB radio. "Pedal to the metal."

Zack didn't buy it. "But we need you back. And I promise I'll never bring a rodent through the lobby again." He had finally admitted the truth to Mr. Moseby.

"That was you?" Mr. Moseby asked. Somehow he had known.

"Yes. And I'm sorry. I'm totally, completely, absolutely sorry. Really, really sorry." Zack meant it.

Mr. Moseby seemed to believe him, too. "Thank you for coming up here and telling me that," he said in his most dignified voice.

"Now, if you'll excuse me, I'm in the middle of a very important project." With that, he lifted the cloth that was draped over a giant structure on the coffee table. This revealed what was clearly a model of the Tipton Hotel, a model he had constructed out of Popsicle sticks. He took the stick he'd been sucking on out of his mouth and added it to the top of the fragile building.

"That's the Tipton," Zack said.

"One one-hundredth scale," Mr. Moseby announced with pride.

"Wow, you got the top of the Tip just right," Zack said, reaching out to touch it.

"Don't—" But Mr. Moseby was too late. The model fell apart just as Zack's finger made contact. "—touch that," Mr. Moseby finished, knowing his warning was of no use now. He just sighed.

There was nothing left for Zack to say,

except that he was sorry, again. He hoped this would be enough for now. Then he headed home, though he couldn't get the thought of all the mess he had caused out of his head.

Chapter 5

That night, Carey came in to say good night to the boys. She sat with Zack for an extralong time. Cody had already fallen asleep, but Zack was upset. "I don't understand," he said to his mom. "I went and apologized to Mr. Moseby, but things still aren't any better."

"Well, it's good that you apologized, but

that doesn't always fix everything." Carey tried to comfort him, but she wanted to be realistic.

"That stinks," Zack said.

"That's life," Carey explained. "Sometimes it takes more than just saying you're sorry. Now, try to get some sleep, okay?"

"Okay," Zack said.

Carey kissed him then and said, "Love you."

"Love you, too," Zack responded.

As soon as Carey was out the door, Zack turned over in his bed to find the long-lost rats sitting on his pillow, looking right at him! "Bonnie! Clyde! Thank goodness you're back!" He scooped them up and ran over to Cody's bed. He had to tell his brother right away. Shaking Cody, Zack said, "Cody, wake up!"

Cody slowly woke up and looked at his

brother. "Are we moving again?" he asked groggily.

"No! Look who came back, Bonnie and Clyde!" Zack was really excited.

"Yes!" Cody was fully awake now. "Oh, thank goodness we found them before the dog party. That would have been a disaster."

"Yeah," Zack said slowly. The beginnings of a plan began to form in his head. "The kind that would get a manager fired. Cody, that's a brilliant plan!"

"Thanks," Cody said proudly. "What's my plan again?"

The boys decided that they had to get started on their plan right away, so Cody headed out to the hallway to make an important call. "Hello, is this the Cat Lovers Society?" he said into the phone in his deepest, most grown-up voice. "Is this the head cat? Well, you and your entire group have just won a free weekend at the Tipton Hotel." He paused, listening to the 'head cat's' question. "Yes, bring as many kitties as you'd like," he said, smiling to himself. He hung up the phone and headed back to bed, but not before he let some excitement out. "Yeah!" he shouted to no one in particular. The plan was in motion.

While Cody was busy making his call, Zack had gone to the basement to get started on his part. There he sat, in front of a big computer panel. He had connected his laptop to the hotel's main computer system and worked his magic. Typing furiously, he said out loud, "Look who's been assigned to a new room. Everybody!"

The next day, the usually serene and pleasant Tipton lobby was in a state of chaos. Ilsa was at her post behind the front desk, trying to field complaints from all the hotel's guests. People were waving room cards in her face angrily, yelling that they were not able to get into their own rooms. Esteban was perched at the computer, doing his best to figure out what could have happened.

"Oh, boy," Ilsa muttered. Then, she uttered her favorite phrase to the crowd of people shouting in her face. "Dut-dut-dut! Put a lederhosen in it, blondie!" She turned to Esteban. "Esteban! What is going on with the computer?"

Esteban had no idea. "Oh, I don't know. Every time I push a button I get a picture of

Zack had a science project to work on with Cody, but he focused on his yo-yoing skills instead. "Look, centrifugal force," he said as he swung his yo-yo.

"Jeny Freiberger just threw the most incredible party for her dog, and Ivana's upset," said London. "I want a bigger, better party for Ivana in the grand ballroom."

"I will take care of it personally," Mr. Moseby said.
But as soon as London left the hotel lobby,
Mr. Moseby asked Maddie to handle the party plans!

"Mr. Moseby!" cried Esteban. "You received a fax!
The Tipton hotel inspector is on the way
for a surprise inspection."

"Aren't you two supposed to be working on your science experiment?" asked the twins' mom. As soon as the boys showed her the rats they were using for their project, she jumped on a chair!

"Mr. Moseby, in my twenty years as a hotel inspector, I have never been so appalled," said Ilsa. "I am taking over the management of this hotel."

"You gotta come back, Mr. Moseby," Zack begged. "Ilsa's a nightmare."
"I'm sorry to hear that," said Mr. Moseby, "but there is nothing
I can do. I have been suspended."

Thanks to Zack and Cody's three-phase plan to get rid of Ilsa,
the Tipton lobby was in chaos when Mr. Moseby walked in.
Soon, he had taken care of everything—including Ilsa!

a koala bear." He stared at the screen with a smile. "And he's doing a dance."

Ilsa was not amused. "Have you tried to restart it?" she asked.

"Oh, only Mr. Moseby knows how," Esteban told her. "I've tried everything."

Ilsa would not have any excuses. "Have you tried this?" she said, pounding on the keyboard with her fist. The computer promptly shut down. She looked at Esteban, accusing him. "Ooh! You have broken it!" She hit him in the arm as punishment and walked away.

Just then, London emerged from the party room with Ivana, both wearing fluffy, skinny purple scarves, along with matching party hats. London pushed her way through the crowd to the front desk and demanded answers. "What's going on out here?" she asked Ilsa. "You're disturbing Ivana's party. They're playing Spin the Milk-Bone."

This was probably the moment when Ilsa started to lose her cool. "I don't have time for your petty puppy problems!" Well this just would not do for London. No one belittled her puppy, or her problems.

She thrust Ivana in Ilsa's face and imitated a fierce dog, "*Grrr! Grrr!*" But of course, this did not scare Ilsa. She didn't even flinch.

"Ha! You don't scare me. I once bit a shark!" she laughed evilly. London backed down from the fight when Maddie entered the lobby. She was in full doggie-clown regalia—furry brown doggie suit, complete with a big, red polka-dot tie, a blackened nose, and whiskers on her face. She felt she had hit a new low.

"London, we have a problem," Maddie said.

"What are you doing out here? You're

supposed to be making balloon people for the dogs," London reprimanded.

"I've had it," Maddie said, exasperated. "Two of your guests bit me and one went tinkle on my leg." London didn't care. She grabbed Maddie and dragged her back toward the party. "No!" Maddie whined. "Don't make me go back in there!"

Next, the cat people arrived, cats in arms. The boys' plan was progressing perfectly! A woman from the group managed to make her way through the throng of angry guests to the desk, where she confronted Ilsa.

"Excuse me, excuse me. We're here for the Cat Lovers convention," the woman said.

"The what?" Ilsa asked.

"We were all promised free rooms. And complimentary litter boxes."

"Let me check that for you," Ilsa said, knowing full well she could not check anything for anyone. She banged on the computer desperately. "I can't seem to find it," she said.

Zack, Cody, and Muriel all huddled together, watching the scene from afar. "Phase one complete," Zack said.

"Phase two: get Mr. Moseby here," Cody replied. At this, Zack dialed his cell phone and made the call to Mr. Moseby. Mr. Moseby, meanwhile, was still in his robe. And he was still working on his Popsicle model of the Tipton Hotel. Once again, he was putting the final stick on his master-piece. When he answered the phone, he forgot himself.

"Tipton Hote—" he started to say. "Moseby residence."

"Mr. Moseby! It's Zack. You gotta get over here! The place is going crazy. We need you!"

"I'm sure Ilsa can handle it."

Zack knew Mr. Moseby might react this way, so he had prepared the group for this kind of resistance. They had to make Mr. Moseby believe that the hotel was in real trouble. They knew that Mr. Moseby loved the place too much to stay away if he thought he might be able to make things right. Zack held the phone up to Esteban, who pretended to be drowning in a flood.

"The water is up to my neck! Losing . . . air . . . fast . . ." he said, gurgling.

"There's water in my hotel?" Mr. Moseby asked, alarmed. It was Muriel's turn next.

"Take your stinkin' paws off of me, you dirty ape!" she demanded.

"There are apes in my hotel?" Mr. Moseby said with worry in his voice.

"Help! There's an angry mob running through the lobby. Look out!" Cody yelled.

Then, for the full effect, he dropped a box full of broken plates on the floor. At the sound of that, Mr. Moseby folded.

"The Tipton needs me! I'm comin', Mama!" he said as he dropped the phone. He threw off his robe, revealing a suit jacket and tie. In all the excitement, he seemed to have forgotten that he had not put pants on, and he raced out the door only half dressed. It only took him a moment to realize, though, and he raced back in, put on a pair of pants, and ran out again.

Back at the hotel, the boys were moving into the next phase of their plan. "On to phase three: release the rats!" Zack said, carrying an empty cage and walking toward the room where Ivana's doggy birthday party was taking place. At the same time, Cody prepared the rats for their mission. "Bonnie, Clyde . . . we've gone over the plan. You know what to do." The rats squeaked. "Remember," Cody said seriously, "we're doing this for Moseby." With that, he opened the cage so it faced the party room, and released them. Bonnie and Clyde scurried right past the front desk, where all the cat lovers stood. The cat lovers and their cats, that is. One of the cats couldn't resist and jumped from his owner's arms, giving chase. Another cat followed suit. Zack waited by the party room with his empty cage, ready to scoop up the rats into safety. The rats ran right into Zack's cage, but the cats kept on running, right into the doggie party! Suddenly, everyone became aware of the yowling and barking of the cats and dogs. Then, all at once, the animals came barreling through the lobby.

"For the love of schnitzel!" Ilsa exclaimed, as the crowd broke into more screaming and yelling themselves. It was mayhem.

Cody and Zack stood by calmly, admiring the scene. Filled with emotion, Cody said to Zack, "This may be some of your best work."

But Zack wasn't convinced. "Only if it gets Mr. Moseby back," he said. What happened next couldn't have been planned any better, except that it wasn't planned at all. It was fate. Three men entered the hotel right in the middle of this madness. One of them spotted Ilsa and approached her skeptically.

"Ms. Schickelgrubermeiger?" he asked. "I'm Ottino Guistefester." Then he motioned to the other men and said their names, by way of introduction. "Ambrose Licarterman. Bob Smith." Apparently, not all of the Tipton inspectors had hard-to-pronounce last names.

"Oh, from the Tipton review board," Ilsa remarked nervously. "Is there any way you can come back . . ." She paused. "Not now?" London's yappy little dog had taken this opportunity to start a fight with Ilsa's pant leg. She was chewing on it viciously when Ilsa yelled, "Get this mangy mutt off of me!"

London sat comfortably by, watching the whole scene with amusement. In her best deadpan voice, she said, "Stop. Bad dog. No."

Just when things couldn't get any worse for Ilsa, Mr. Moseby rushed in. "Good gracious! What is going on here?!" he asked. Zack and Cody couldn't have planned it better.

"Perfect timing," Zack said. Starting another round of their chasing game, the dogs came running through and were about to pass by Mr. Moseby, when he held out his hand, defying them to go any further.

"Dogs, halt!" he said in a deep, controlled voice. Immediately, the dogs stopped at Mr. Moseby's feet. Maddie—who had come running after them, yelling, "Wait! Stop! You forgot your doggie bags!"—stopped, too.

"Sit!" Mr. Moseby ordered, and they all sat . . . even Maddie. "Now go back to your party. There's nothing to see here," he said with authority. All of them, even Maddie, exited the room obediently. But as Maddie crawled back toward the party room, she found herself at Mr. Moseby's feet. He gave her a look, and she quickly got up, smoothed her doggie clown suit, and walked away with what was left of her dignity.

"Ladies and gentlemen, may I have your attention, please." Mr. Moseby was taking control. "All your complaints will be handled immediately." He approached a Japanese guest and said, in Japanese, "Ah, Mr. Takamoto, our humblest apologies. Dinner is on me." Then, he turned to Mademoiselle Chantal, and spoke to her in French. "Allow me to upgrade you to a suite." Then, he said to an African man in his native tongue, "Mr. Moombassa, free tickets to *Hairspray*."

To which Mr. Moombassa replied in English, "Cool."

Mr. Moseby wasn't finished restoring order just yet. "Esteban!" he called to his loyal friend.

Esteban hurried over and said, "Yes, your majesty."

"I want gift baskets for each of these guests immediately. And some catnip for our feline friends."

"For you, anything!" Esteban vowed and ran off. As he passed Ilsa, he said, "For you, bubkes."

Observing all this, Mr. Guistefester said, "Mr. Moseby, on behalf of the Tipton review board, I must say, I am very impressed."

"Thank you, sir," Mr. Moseby replied.

Ilsa felt the need to defend herself now. "I'll have you know, I had everything under control."

"Not from where we stand," Mr. Guistefester said. "I think this review is done. You obviously can't inspire loyalty in a staff, and you certainly are not fit to run a hotel."

Ilsa was outraged. "This isn't a hotel— this is a circus! There's dogs and cats and rats and clowns and twins! The only thing missing is a bearded lady!" Realizing that Mr. Moseby was staring at her mole, she said, "Watch it! You'd have to be out of your mind to work here!"

"Well, then call me crazy," Mr. Moseby said happily.

"Mr. Moseby, please continue your fine work," Mr. Guistefester said before turning his attention to Ilsa. Extending his open hand to her, he said, "Ms. Schickelgrubermeiger, your Tipton keys, your name tag, and your pen." Ilsa handed them over at once, making sure to stab him with the pen.

"Ow!" Mr. Guistefester yelped.

Mr. Moseby, always a gentleman, offered a hand to Ilsa. "No hard feelings," he said. But just as she reached out to shake, he pulled his hand away. "Psych!" Okay, so he wasn't *always* a gentleman.

"I'll get you next time, Mr. Moseby." Looking hard at London, she said, "And your little dog, too!" She sounded just like the Wicked Witch of the West! She made her way to the front door, and the doorman, rather than open the door for her, simply stood there, arms crossed. This was met with loud applause from the entire staff of the Tipton Hotel.

"Dut-dut-dut!" she said for the last time, and then she pushed her way past the doorman in frustration. At last, she was gone.

Mr. Moseby was standing with Zack and Cody. "Was all of this your doing?" he asked.

Cody pointed to his brother. "It was Zack," he said.

"I'm sorry, Mr. Moseby," Zack blurted out earnestly.

"So you engineered this mayhem, nearly destroying my hotel in the process?" Mr. Moseby asked.

"Yes, I did," Zack admitted.

"I just have one thing to say to you, young man," Mr. Moseby said. Zack braced himself. "Thank you."

Zack smiled with relief. "My pleasure."

Cody wanted some credit here. "Hey, hey! I helped destroy the hotel, too," he said.

"You know, boys, next week the health inspector is coming. You ever been to New York?"

"Throw in Yankee tickets and we're there." Zack cheered. Order had been restored to the Tipton Hotel, and life was good.

For Maddie, though, the day wasn't over just yet. There was the business of the poker party that had to be addressed. Just when she thought it couldn't get any worse for her, she found herself sitting around a poker table with a bunch of dogs.

Still in her costume, Maddie held five cards in her hand. She studied them carefully. "I'm going to see your bet and raise you two," she said to one of the dogs. She figured she might as well give this job her all. She tossed in three chips to show the dogs she was serious, and one of them whimpered. "Oh, hush up," she told the dog. "Put your bones in or fold."

The dog had to fold. There was no messing with Maddie—she had had a terrible day. "Ha-ha!" she laughed, raking in all the chips. "Roll over and weep!"

Keeping Secrets

Adapted by Beth Beechwood

Based on the television series, "Hannah Montana", created by Michael Poryes and Rich Correll & Barry O'Brien

Based on the episode written by Michael Poryes

Chapter One

The crowd was going wild after the
Hannah Montana concert. But all Hannah
could think about was getting offstage
and taking off her wig! Then she could go

63

back to being Miley Stewart. Miley was so glad she hadn't told her friends that Hannah Montana—the pop star they were all crazy for—was really just her in disguise! She enjoyed knowing that her friends liked her for who she was, not because she was famous. Only her dad, her brother, and her best friend, Lilly, knew the truth.

"Clear the way, clear the way! Superstar coming through!" Miley's dad, Robby Stewart, shouted to the crowd as he, Miley, and Lilly hurried toward the limo. They all had to wear disguises in order to protect Miley's secret. Lilly was dressed as her alias Lola Luftnagle, and carrying a little Goth lapdog named Thor. Mr. Stewart was in his "Hannah's manager" disguise.

Miley, still dressed as Hannah Montana,

always made sure to show her appreciation to the fans. She turned to the crowd and smiled broadly. "Thank you, everybody!" Her strong voice carried the words like a song. "Love to you all! See you next time!"

Though Lilly knew how popular Hannah was, it always surprised her to be in the thick of it. "This is totally insane!" Then, holding Thor up to the crowd, she yelled, "Back off, people! Back off—don't make me release Thor!"

"Yeah," Miley said, smiling at her brave defender. "You go get 'em, Thor. Two pounds of pure piddle just lookin' for a target."

Looking down and nodding at the puddle surrounding his feet, Mr. Stewart said, "Actually, I think he just found one."

Lilly was embarrassed. "Oh, man!" she

cried as they piled into the limo and closed the door. Only, the window was still half open and they could hear someone shouting, "Hold up! Wait!" It was Oliver Oken, Hannah Montana's number one fan.

"Oh, no," moaned Miley. "It's Oliver. *Again*. He snuck into my dressing room last week. He nearly climbed onstage the week before. Just when I think he can't get any more obsessed, *BAM!*, he kicks it up a notch!"

Mr. Stewart was entertained, though. "Look at those bony little elbows go!" he said as Oliver made his way through the throngs. "That boy cuts through a crowd like a Weedwacker."

Miley was anxious. "Close the window!" she commanded. Lilly responded swiftly and the window almost zipped shut, but not before Oliver could thrust his hand inside and stop it from closing all the way.

"Hannah, please!" Oliver begged. "Kiss my hand and I'll never wash it again."

Miley rolled her eyes. "Looks like he never washed it now." Thinking fast, she took Thor from Lilly and poised him right at Oliver's grimy hand. "Come on, Thor, make yourself useful."

Thor gave Oliver's hand a big lick. Fooled, Oliver was beside himself. "Oh, baby, that was a wet one!"

Even when Miley slapped Oliver's hand out of the way, he was not discouraged.

"Ooh, I like 'em feisty," Oliver swooned as he pulled his hand away. Lilly was able to close the window at long last, and Mr. Stewart turned to the driver.

"You can head out," he said.

Miley was exasperated. "Man," she sighed. "He's never gonna give up."

Lilly got serious. "You better hope he does. Because if he ever finds out your secret, he'll not only be in love with Hannah Montana, he'll be in love with you!"

Miley looked at her friend incredulously. "What? That's crazy! The only thing that's the same about Hannah Montana and me is—" Miley paused for a moment until she realized the truth. "—me." She gathered herself again. "And 'me' doesn't feel that way about him!"

Her dad, however, quickly reassured her. "Don't worry, Mile, I know guys, and sooner or later he'll get tired of chasing after someone who doesn't chase back." But they all realized it would probably be later rather than sooner. This was Oliver they were talking about. And everyone knew Oliver never gave up.

Just then, Mr. Stewart opened the window only to find Oliver furiously peddling his bike alongside the limo. He clutched a small bouquet of flowers in his hand, and as they began to disintegrate in the wind, he shouted, "Do a dude a favor and don't get on the freeway!" But the limo sped up, and Oliver finally started to fall behind, throwing the flowers through the limo window in a last-ditch effort to impress Hannah. "For you, my love!"

Miley shook her head at Thor. "Why did you have to be such a good kisser?"

Chapter Two

The next day at Rico's, a beach hangout, Oliver was holding court with all the guys, telling them the tall tale of "Hannah's" hand kiss. Miley and Lilly had just arrived from the beach, when they overheard Oliver's story. Even Chad the Chomper, who had been busy shooting hoops, stopped long enough to listen.

"It's true," Oliver insisted to the guys. "Hannah actually kissed this hand," he said, pointing to an imaginary spot.

"You gotta be kidding me," said one of the guys he was talking to.

Oliver would not entertain doubters. "A big, slobbery wet one," he said enthusiastically. "Look, it's still shiny."

Lilly couldn't resist. She whispered to Miley, "Yeah, and now every time Oliver calls my house, my dog goes, 'Is it for me, is it for me?'" The girls giggled at their inside joke.

"Chad, dude, close up shop when you chew," Oliver demanded. Chad was chomping on gum a little too dramatically for Oliver's liking. "You're getting spit on the Hannah hand!" Chad wasn't about to listen to Oliver, though. Instead, he shoved another piece of gum into his mouth and chewed even louder. Oliver moved his hand away to protect his precious doggy kiss.

Lilly had had enough. "Mile, let's go. You're cutting into my tan time."

But Miley was distracted. "Look at him, he's never gonna quit. What happens if he does find out? I really care about Oliver. It'd totally weird out our friendship."

Lilly became a little suspicious of her friend, suddenly. "Unless deep, deep down, maybe, just maybe, you feel the same way . . ." They both glanced over at Oliver, who was busy stroking the side of his face with the part of his hand "Hannah" had kissed. The image shook Miley back into reality. "Yes, and maybe, just maybe . . . that's insane!" They laughed and looked on as Oliver continued with his fantasy story.

"Now that she's left her mark on me, it's time to take our relationship to the next level," Oliver said. "Tonight at her CD signing, I'll stare into her eyes and say, 'You're my love, my life, someday you'll be my . . .'" He paused for a moment and stared at the sky, deep in thought. Then, he started to write on his hand, *"Note to self: think of word that rhymes with 'life.'"* Just then, one of the guys pointed out something pretty crucial to Oliver.

"Dude, isn't that the Hannah hand?"

Oliver screamed, "AHHHHH!" Looking sorrowfully down at his hand, he pined, "Forgive me, my love."

The whole incident reminded Miley of something she had forgotten, too. "The CD signing! If he stares into my eyes, he might totally recognize me."

Lilly didn't buy it and brushed off the possibility. "It's never gonna happen."

Miley was still concerned. "But what if it does?"

Lilly looked at her friend seriously. "Then you'll learn to love him like I did with my brother's hamster. And here's the beauty part: if Oliver dies, you won't have to bury him in your backyard."

Sometimes Miley couldn't believe she even knew Lilly. "When you talk, do you hear it, or is there, like, this big roaring in your ears?"

Meanwhile, Oliver was getting more and more irritated as Chad chewed his gum. Chad, clearly amused by this, moved even closer to Oliver's ear and chomped even louder.

"Step off, Chad!" Oliver yelled.

Chad agreed. "Fine. Toss this for me, would ya?" With that, Chad took the wad of gum from his mouth and slapped it down, right on Oliver's precious Hannah hand.

Oliver couldn't take it. "Get it off," he screamed. "Get it off!"

One of the guys to whom Oliver had been bragging earlier looked on curiously. "What's the deal with you and gum chewing?" he asked Oliver.

Suddenly, Oliver was lost in the blurry past. He was back in his crib. He was a baby, and all he could remember was an older woman, his Aunt Harriet, leaning over him, chomping on gum. *Chomp, chomp, chomp.* "Look at you, little Ollie," he recalled her saying while she chomped. "Aunt Harriet wants to eat you up." *Chomp, chomp, chomp.* "You're just so yummy, darling . . . yummy, yummy, yummy."

Oliver cringed as he remembered what happened next. Aunt Harriet's gum had fallen right out of her mouth with the last "yummy"—right out of her mouth and onto a very disgusted little Ollie. Oliver shook himself back to the present at Rico's.

"I hate that woman," he said out loud to no one in particular.

Collect all the books in this royally fun pony series!

by Diana Kimpton

HYPERION
BOOKS FOR CHILDREN